Peter Spier's
RAIN

To Nancy and Bob Banker: May your skies be clear and
your days be filled with sunshine!

Peter Spier's
RAIN

Published by Bantam Doubleday Dell Books for Young Readers
a division of Bantam Doubleday Dell Publishing Group, Inc., 1540 Broadway, New York, New York 10036

Illustrations copyright © 1982 by Peter Spier

ISBN: 0-440-41347-8
Reprinted by arrangement with Doubleday Books for Young Readers
Printed in the United States of America
April 1997   10 9 8 7 6 5 4 3 2

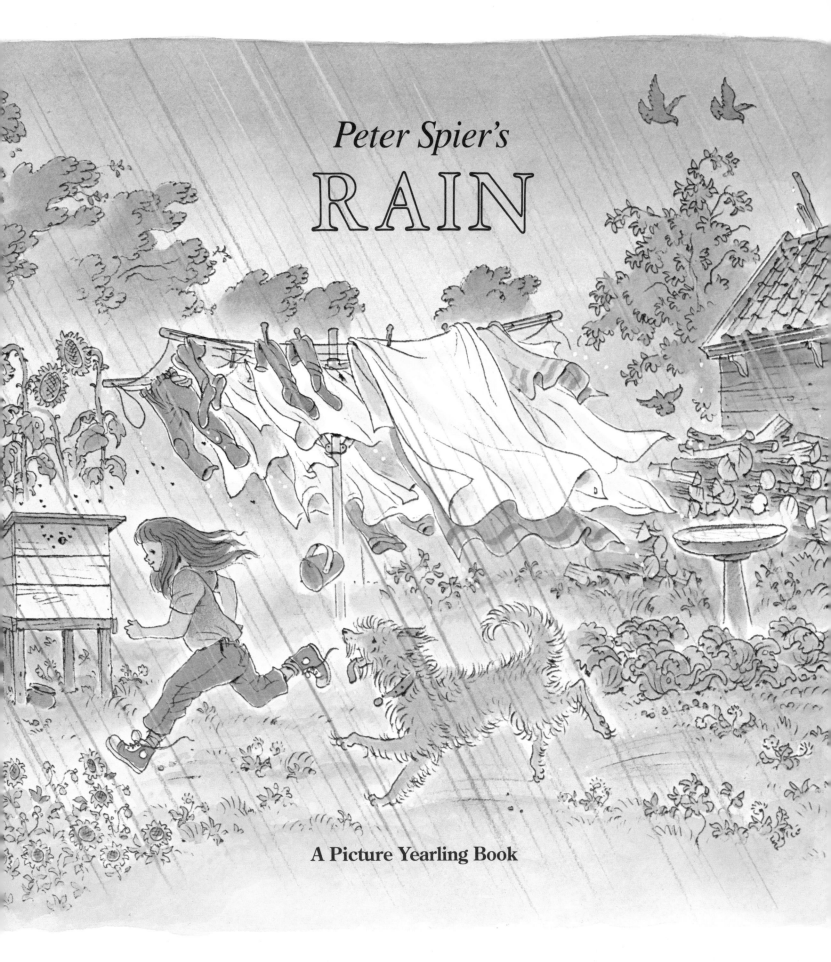

Peter Spier's
RAIN

A Picture Yearling Book